HE MYSTERY AT THE BALLPARK

created by
GERTRUDE CHANDLER WARNER

Illustrated by Charles Tang

ALBERT WHITMAN & Company
Morton Grove, Illinois

Activities by Nancy E. Krulik

Activity illustrations by Alfred Giuliani

ISBN 0-8075-5341-7

5 7 9 10 8 6

Printed in the U.S.A.

Contents

CHAPTER 1

Tryouts

"But I'm not very good at base-ball," Violet said to Henry. It was early evening and the Aldens were sitting on their front porch in Greenfield.

Henry, who was fourteen, gave his sister an encouraging smile. "Don't worry, Violet. All you need is a little practice." Ten-year-old Violet was a shy girl with long brown hair and a sweet personality.

"I'm excited!" Jessie said. "I was hoping someone would start a team in Greenfield."

"Who told you about it?" Violet asked.

"Michael and Nicole Parker," Henry said. "They just moved in down the street. They said the real estate agent told them about the team!"

"We have new kids to play with?" Benny asked excitedly. He tucked his legs under the porch swing and set it rocking. "How old are they?" Benny, age six, loved to make new friends.

"Michael's twelve and Nicole is ten," Jessie said. "They want us to go to the dugout with them tomorrow morning."

"What's a dugout?" Benny asked.

"That's the little shelter where the players sit while they wait for their turn to bat," Jessie explained.

"Are Michael and Nicole really good at baseball?" Violet asked. She still felt a little uncertain about playing.

"I don't think so," Jessie said, hoping to reassure her sister. "I think they just want to make friends with all the kids in the neighborhood."

"I think we should do it," Henry said. "It will be fun!"

"I want to be a pitcher," Benny chimed in. He jumped off the swing and threw an imaginary ball.

"It's too bad Soo Lee is away," Jessie pointed out. "She likes sports." Soo Lee was their cousin, and she had gone fishing with her father.

"I think it's time for us to make a trip into town to get you some equipment," their grandfather said, rising from his chair. Watch, the family dog, scampered happily toward the driveway. He loved riding in the car with the children.

"Yippee!" Benny grabbed Grandfather's hand. "Can I buy a baseball cap, too?"

"Of course," Grandfather said.

"We should make a list of what we need," Jessie said thoughtfully. Jessie was twelve and always liked to plan ahead.

"I can use my Hank Aaron glove," Jessie said excitedly. Aunt Jane had given Jessie the old autographed glove for her birthday, and Jessie treasured it. Although it was a little too large, she used it whenever she had the chance.

"I think a ball and bat will be enough," Henry said. "Mr. Warren said that the kids share equipment."

"Who's Mr. Warren?" Benny asked. He jumped in the front seat the moment Grandfather opened the car door.

"That's the coach. Michael met him earlier today," Henry explained.

"We have a real coach!" Benny was thrilled. He was going to be part of a team!

The next morning was bright and clear as the Aldens gathered around the kitchen table. "I want everyone to have a good breakfast," Mrs. McGregor said, passing Benny a plate of pancakes. Mrs. McGregor was the Aldens' housekeeper and had been taking care of the family for years.

"These look good!" Benny loved to eat. He filled his plate with pancakes and scrambled eggs.

Jessie noticed four new water bottles sitting on the kitchen counter. "Thanks for filling those with ice water," she said to Mrs.

McGregor. "I was going to do that after breakfast."

"You can help me finish the lunches if you'd like," Mrs. McGregor said.

"What are we having?" Benny asked, eyeing the clock. He decided he had time for one more glass of orange juice.

"All your favorites." Mrs. McGregor checked the brown paper bags. "Peanut butter and jelly sandwiches, apples, and brownies."

Benny grinned and pushed back his chair. "I can hardly wait till lunch!"

Ten minutes later, the Parker children knocked on the front door. Michael was tall with a friendly smile. His sister, Nicole, stood beside him, her long hair pulled back in a ponytail.

"Ready to go?" Michael asked.

"Yes we are," said Jessie eagerly. She and Henry had been throwing a ball around as they waited.

"Ready as I'll ever be," Violet said uncertainly. She was still a bit nervous.

"I know how you feel," said Nicole. "I'm not much of a ballplayer either."

When they reached the field, they found a large group of children milling around. Violet noticed that all the girls and boys seemed to be at least ten years old. She glanced down at Benny. Was he too young to play? He was very proud of the bat and ball Grandfather had bought him, and she didn't want him to be disappointed.

Just then, a tall, sandy-haired young man approached them. "Hi there. I'm Chuck Roberts, the assistant coach." He was carrying a clipboard and had a pencil tucked behind his ear. "I need your name, age, and what position you want to play. Let's start with you." He pointed to Nicole.

"Ohmigosh." Nicole looked flustered. "I'm Nicole Parker, I'm ten years old, and . . ." she glanced at her brother. "What position do I want to play?"

"You haven't played much baseball, right?" Chuck was looking at her thoughtfully.

"Neither have I," Benny piped up. He

tossed his ball in the air and caught it. "It looks like fun, though."

"It is." Chuck handed the clipboard to Nicole. "Just write down your names and ages, and I'll tell Coach Warren we've got some beginners."

"How do we know what position to play?" Nicole asked curiously.

"It all depends on what you're good at," Chuck said.

"What do you mean?" Benny looked up, squinting his eyes in the bright sunlight.

"Well, if you have a strong arm, you might want to be a third baseman, but if you've got quick feet and quick hands, you might want to play second base." Chuck waited while Benny carefully printed his name. "Does anyone know what a shortstop is?"

"The shortest person on the team?" Benny offered.

Everyone laughed. "The shortstop stands between second and third base," Jessie called out.

"That's right," said Chuck.

"I have a lot to learn," Nicole said. She

traced a circle in the dust with the head of her bat.

"Don't worry, that's what we're here for." Chuck started to move away, but Benny tugged on his arm.

"What do we do next?" he asked.

"After you've signed up, get in line for tryouts," Chuck told him.

"Tryouts?" Nicole and Violet exchanged a look.

Nicole was worried. "If this is a test," she muttered, "I sure hope I pass."

The Aldens, along with Michael and Nicole, lined up as Coach Warren led the tryouts. He watched carefully as the children took turns pitching.

"Remember," Chuck called to a shy-looking girl, "you need to throw hard, and you need to throw with confidence." He waited until she pitched three balls in a row and then pointed to Violet. "You're next."

Violet gulped. The new ball felt slippery in her hands, and she dropped it as she moved into position.

"Just a second," Chuck said, walking toward her. "Do you have a good grip on the ball?"

Violet looked up nervously, clutching the baseball tightly.

"Hey, relax," Chuck said. "Look, this is how you throw the ball." He demonstrated for her.

"Oh no!" Violet cried as her ball went only a few feet and then dropped to the ground.

"That's okay." Chuck looked sympathetic. "You'll get the hang of it in a few days. You just need some practice." He walked back toward Coach Warren.

Next it was Jessie's turn. She pitched three balls, and even though they didn't go as far as she wanted them to, Chuck seemed satisfied.

"I wish I could pitch like that," someone said behind her a moment later.

Jessie recognized the shy-looking girl who had been pitching before. "Thanks. I play a lot — I love baseball." She stuck out her hand. "I'm Jessie."

"My name's Ann." She had pale skin, with tiny freckles sprinkled across her nose. "I just hope I do better at hitting than I did at pitching."

"That's a nice bat you have."

"Thanks. It belonged to my father. See all these little notches?" She ran her hand along the polished surface. "Each one means he got a home run."

"Wow." Jessie peered at the bat. "He was a good hitter!" She glanced over at Violet who was standing at home plate, wielding her new baseball bat. "That's my sister," she said, nodding toward the field. They watched as Violet swung and missed three balls in a row. Jessie sighed. "I don't think she's got the hang of this yet."

"She'll be fine," Ann said. Both girls cheered when Violet hit the fourth ball with a loud whack. "See what I mean?" Ann asked with a grin.

"Lunch break, everyone!" Chuck Roberts yelled.

Jessie and Ann began walking around the edge of the field toward some picnic tables in the shade.

"I'll introduce you to the rest of my family," Jessie offered. "And to two new friends of ours."

"I'd like that," Ann said quietly. "I don't know anyone here."

"You will," Jessie assured her. "Just remember, we're a team!"

CHAPTER 2

A Special Job for Benny

"Do you think we'll make the team?" Jessie passed Benny a water bottle and watched as he tore into his peanut butter and jelly sandwich. All of the kids were sitting at picnic tables having lunch.

"I'm already on the team. I'm a batboy," Benny said proudly. He wasn't exactly sure what that meant, but he knew it was an important job.

"Benny's going to be helping Mr. Jackson, who's in charge of the equipment," Henry explained. Benny was too young to play on the team, so Coach Warren had decided to give him a special job to do.

"That will be lots of fun, Benny." Violet was happy that her younger brother was going to be included, but she wondered if he would like working with Mr. Jackson. She had met him a few minutes earlier and he seemed like a very cranky old man.

"But what about the rest of us?" Jessie persisted. "Do you think we have a chance?"

"I don't think I do," Ann said sadly. "I didn't pitch very well, and I missed two balls when it was my turn to bat."

"Don't be discouraged, Ann. Trying is what counts." Henry reached for one of Mrs. McGregor's brownies. "Chuck told me that Coach Warren looks for kids who are good team players. That's even more important than talent."

"What about you, Henry?" Michael spoke up. "I didn't see you doing any pitching or hitting today."

"I'm not going to be on the team," Henry began.

"What!" Violet was crushed. How could

her big brother not make the team! He was much stronger than anyone else on the field.

Henry chuckled. "Relax, Violet. I'm not going to be on the team, but I'm going to be part of it." He paused and looked around the table. "They decided that since I'm older than the other kids, I could help out. So I'm going to be Chuck's assistant."

"Wow!" Benny's eyes were wide with excitement. He was very proud of his brother.

"Then you can tell us what's going on," Nicole said. She twisted a lock of dark curly hair in her fingers. "Are they going to make the announcements after lunch, or will there be more tryouts?"

"No, tryouts are over. Chuck said that he and Coach Warren are going to go over the notes during lunch and come to a final decision."

"I feel nervous," Ann said quietly.

"Me, too," Nicole agreed. She looked at her brother, Michael, and knew that he was thinking the same thing. Now that they had made some new friends, they didn't want to lose them!

"Ready for some work?" Chuck appeared and patted Benny on the back. "I could use some help with the equipment."

"Sure thing!" Benny wolfed down the last bite of brownie and scrambled to his feet.

"Have you — I mean, has Coach Warren made up his mind yet?" Violet was so nervous her heart was thumping.

"He's still working on it," Chuck said casually. "We're going to post the list in half an hour or so, so you can relax for now."

"Relax!" Nicole blurted out. "You've got to be kidding!"

"Let's go, Benny. I'm going to give you your very first job to do."

"I'm ready!" Benny swung his legs off the bench and leaped to his feet. This was going to be fun!

They walked to the dugout, a small building that was open on one side to the field. Benches lined the open side, where the players sat during the game. Inside the dugout were several metal lockers and a cabinet to hold the equipment. Mr. Jackson sat on a bench inside, cleaning a glove with an oily rag. He was tall and thin, with wavy gray hair. He wasn't very friendly. When Chuck introduced Benny, he grumbled hello and then went back to what he was doing.

"Do you know much about baseball equipment?" Chuck asked.

"I know you need a ball and bat," Benny said.

"There's something else you need," Chuck said seriously, "and that's a batting helmet. Coach Warren wants everyone on the team to have one by tomorrow, and we're going to keep them in here." He pointed to a wooden cabinet. "For your first job, why don't you dust the shelves." He handed Benny a soft white cloth.

"Why do we need helmets?" Benny said, working quickly. He was glad that Chuck had chosen him to help out and wanted to do well.

"To protect your head when you're at bat or running the bases," Chuck explained. "You don't want to get hit by a ball." He coughed as a cloud of dust drifted up in his face.

"Sorry," Benny said. "These shelves are really dirty."

"That's okay. They haven't been touched since last season."

"There's an old bat in here," Benny said. He lifted it out and examined the knob. "Look, it must be a lucky bat. It has a number seven on it."

Chuck laughed. "It might be someone's lucky bat, but that's not what the number seven means. It means that the bat is twenty-seven inches long. That's about the right size for most kids."

Benny looked surprised. "I didn't know they came in sizes."

"They sure do. Never buy a bat that's too long. They weigh more, and they're hard to swing quickly."

"I'll remember that," Benny said eagerly. He loved working with Chuck. He was going to learn a lot!

"And buy a wooden bat. Aluminum bats cost a lot and you'll be changing bats as you get bigger."

"Right!"

"And never, never try to bat without your helmet. Coach Warren will really drum that into you."

"Got it!"

On the field, a blonde-haired girl walked over to the other Aldens as they were finishing their lunch. "Hi, I'm Susan Miller," she said with a friendly smile.

Henry scooted over for her to sit down, and everyone introduced themselves. "I saw you pitching before," he said. "You were very good."

"Thanks. I played a lot of baseball at camp last summer." She looked at Violet and Nicole. "What positions do you play?"

Violet looked embarrassed and Nicole giggled. "We're just beginners," Nicole explained. "We're laughing because people have been asking us that all morning."

"Sorry," Susan said. "I guess Coach Warren will figure out where to put everyone."

"Susan! Susan! I've been looking all over for you!" A tall woman rushed over to the table. Behind her was a woman who looked just like her except for her dark curly hair.

"Hi, Mom. Hi, Aunt Edna. I was just getting to know some of the kids." She introduced her mother and aunt to everyone at the table. Jessie noticed that Susan seemed a little downcast when her mother appeared, and suddenly got very quiet. Her mother, however, never stopped talking and asked everyone their names, ages, and how much playing experience they had.

"Are you one of Coach Warren's assistants?" Nicole asked.

Mrs. Miller's jaw dropped. "Why no, why would you ask that?" She flushed a little and Violet knew that she didn't like the question.

Nicole calmly answered, "You seem so interested in everything. I thought maybe you were helping to choose the team."

"Well, I . . . of course not!" Mrs. Miller said abruptly. "I'm just a parent." She put her arm around Susan. "My daughter is an excellent player, and I'm here to watch the tryouts." She looked impatiently toward a folding table where Coach Warren and Chuck were poring over scribbled pages of notes. "I wish they'd hurry up and make up their minds."

"Mom, this takes time," Susan said quietly. "They want to make sure they pick the right people for the right positions."

"How long can it take?" Mrs. Miller snapped. "I can think of several positions that you could play."

Susan managed to change the topic and Jessie was relieved. It was obvious that Mrs. Miller liked having things her way!

"Do you want to walk around the field with me?" Ann stood up. "I'd like to walk some laps while we wait for the news. It makes me edgy just sitting doing nothing."

"Sure, I'll come with you," Nicole said, gathering up her napkin and paper cup.

"Me, too," Violet said, jumping to her feet. Being around Mrs. Miller was making her very nervous.

"How do you like Greenfield so far?" Violet asked Nicole a few minutes later. The three girls were walking briskly around the outer edge of the field. Each one knew that if she were chosen for the team, she'd soon be running two or three miles along the same path every day.

"I like it a lot since we met all of you," Nicole said. "I thought it would take a long time to make new friends, but Michael said joining this team was a good way to get started."

"I'm glad he thought of it," Violet said. "But we'll still be friends, whether we make the team or not."

"Oh, I hope we do," Ann said suddenly. She stopped and peeled off her jacket. "I'm going to put this with my bat, and I'll catch up with you later, okay?" When she left, Nicole told Violet about her family, and Violet told her all about Grandfather and how he had found the Aldens living in a boxcar.

Nicole looked surprised. "You mean you were orphans, living on your own?"

Violet nodded. "We thought we wouldn't like our grandfather, but then he found us and took us into his house, and everything changed. He's the best grandfather in the whole world," she said. "We have a wonderful home, and a dog named Watch, and a really nice housekeeper, Mrs. McGregor, to take care of us."

"They're announcing the team!" a boy said, whizzing by them.

"Oh, let's hurry." The three girls jogged to the center of the field where Chuck was standing with his clipboard. Coach Warren was at his side, and he leaned over and whispered something in Chuck's ear. Chuck nodded, and then motioned for everyone to gather around him.

"First, I want to thank everyone for coming. I know you all tried your hardest."

Jessie glanced over at her sister, and noticed that she had her fingers crossed and had squeezed her eyes tightly shut. Jessie hoped that they would all be playing baseball together the following day.

"We have the final team list," Chuck said. "Anybody who isn't chosen for the team can still be a substitute player. They'll fill in if anyone gets sick or drops out." He shaded his eyes from the sun. "Okay, here goes: Alden . . ."

"Which one?" Violet blurted out, opening her eyes.

Chuck glanced at his list. "Both," he said. "Jessie and Violet."

"Yippee!" Jessie threw her arms around her sister. "We made it!" Both girls were still hugging each other when they heard Nicole's name called out. "Great! We'll all be together!" Jessie said, pulling Nicole into the circle.

"Michael Parker . . . Susan Miller . . . Ann Richmond . . ."

Violet was glad that the shy girl had made the team.

"Where *is* Ann?" Jessie asked.

"Look, there she is." Nicole pointed to Ann, who was running across the field toward them. Nicole started waving, and then stopped and frowned. "Something's wrong. She's crying!"

"Ann, what is it?" Jessie asked when Ann

reached them. Ann's eyes were red, and her face was streaked with tears.

"My dad's bat . . ." she sobbed. "It's gone! I think someone *stole* it!"

"Oh Ann, I'm so sorry," Nicole said. "We'll help you get it back."

Jessie and Violet exchanged a look. The Aldens had another mystery to solve!

CHAPTER 3

The Search

"Tell me exactly where you left it, Ann," Jessie said calmly. "We'll all work together and look until we find it." Jessie knew how important the bat was to Ann.

"I left it in the dugout," Ann said tearfully. "Chuck said it was okay to put our things in that big wooden cabinet."

"We'll spread out," Jessie said, scanning the field. The field was crowded with parents and kids making their way back to their cars. "Violet, why don't you get Benny and Henry to help you search the picnic area?" She turned to Nicole and Michael. "Could you two check the dugout again? Ann and I will cover the field."

Jessie and Ann walked quickly toward the center of the field, weaving in and out of the crowd. Twenty minutes later, Ann was ready to give up. "It's no use. We've gone over every inch of ground," Ann said, sniffling.

Henry and Benny caught up with them. Jessie knew from the look on their faces that they hadn't had any luck either.

Henry spoke first. "I'm sorry, Ann. We looked everywhere." He shrugged helplessly. "It seems to have vanished into thin air."

"We even asked Coach Warren and Chuck," Benny piped up. "And Mr. Jackson."

"No one even saw it?" Ann cried. "What am I going to tell my father?"

"It still might show up," Violet said, hugging Ann. "Someone might have taken it by mistake, and he or she will bring it back tomorrow."

* * *

That night at dinner, the Aldens celebrated with Grandfather. "I'm very proud of all of you," he said, looking around the table. "Two baseball players, a batboy, and an assistant coach."

"Not quite an assistant coach," Henry said, smiling, "but thank you, Grandfather."

"Did you learn much about baseball today, Benny?" Grandfather asked.

"I know I need a lot more practice," Benny said, reaching for a breadstick. "Chuck pitched some balls to me and I swung at them, but I didn't hit any."

"You know, I played a little baseball in my day," Grandfather said. "Maybe I can give you a few pointers before it gets dark."

"Yippee! Let's go!" Benny was ready to scramble off his chair, but Mrs. McGregor stopped him.

"Not so fast, young man. You wouldn't want to miss my hot apple pie with ice cream, would you?"

Grandfather laughed at the look on Benny's face. "Don't worry, Benny, we have time to do both. Enjoy your pie."

Later, at bedtime, Benny told Henry about all the tips Grandfather had given him. He had learned so many things! "Do you know what it means if you swing high one time and low the next time?"

"That you should play another position?" Henry teased him.

Benny made a face. "That you're probably closing your eyes. Grandfather was right. That's exactly what I was doing!"

"It's getting late, Benny," Henry said mildly. He knew his younger brother was very wound up. Benny really loved to talk!

"And do you know what else? It's okay to be afraid of getting hit by the ball."

"Is that so?" Henry asked.

Benny nodded. "Even major league players are afraid of getting hit." He yawned, and scooted down under the covers. "But you have to watch the pitcher, and when the pitcher throws the ball, watch the ball." He pulled the quilt up under his chin. "You have to watch the ball all the way. . . . to the bat." Benny's voice trailed off.

"I'll remember that," Henry said softly. Benny was sound asleep. Tomorrow was going to be a big day for all of them.

The next morning, Coach Warren divided the team into groups. Jessie, Ann, and Nicole found themselves working on fielding drills.

"Okay, everyone!" Chuck blew a sharp blast on his whistle. "You already know how to catch . . ."

"We do?" Ann muttered under her breath. She was upset because she still hadn't found her missing bat.

"So what I'm going to teach you is fielding, or getting ready to catch," Chuck continued.

"I just hope this is easier than pitching," Jessie whispered to Ann.

"One thing you can be sure of," Chuck went on, "baseballs are almost never hit right at the fielder." He casually tossed a ball in the air and caught it. "So that means you have to be ready to move. The best way to get ready is to face the batter. Stand with your feet apart, as far apart as the width of your shoulders."

Jessie took a step out to the side and hunkered down a little.

"That's good, Jessie," Chuck said. "Lean forward a bit. And Nicole, keep your weight on the balls of your feet."

"I don't know if I'll ever get the hang of this," Nicole said an hour and a half later. They were sprawled under an oak tree taking a break before learning some new drills.

"I never thought water could taste this good," Ann said, taking a long, cool drink. Susan Miller walked by, swinging her bat, and Ann suddenly sat bolt upright. "That's my bat!" she said under her breath.

"What?" Jessie looked up in surprise.

"My bat! Susan has my father's bat."

Ann started to scramble to her feet, but Nicole held her back. "Wait a minute. How can you be sure?"

"I'd recognize it anywhere," Ann said, her eyes flashing.

"But why would Susan take it?" Jessie said. "Her mother bought her all new equipment. Anyway, I can't believe she'd take something that didn't belong to her."

"I can't let her get away with it," Ann said, flinging Nicole's hand off her arm.

"Wait a minute. Let's make sure before you confront her." Jessie glanced over her shoulder. They waited until Susan set the bat against a tree and headed for the pay phone. "Now's our chance," Jessie said, as the three girls dashed across the field.

"She put tape on it," Ann said a minute later. She was clutching the bat, picking at a strip of thick black tape. "But this is it all right. Here are the notches underneath."

"Was she trying to disguise it?" Nicole asked.

"Maybe not," Jessie said. "Sometimes people put tape on the bat where they grip it."

"What do we do now?" Ann said quietly. "Susan's on her way back."

"We have to give her a chance to explain," Jessie said.

"This better be good," Ann said. She was clutching the bat tightly to her chest.

"Hi, everybody," Susan said.

Ann got right to the point. "This is my

bat," she said flatly. "I'd like to know how you got it."

Susan looked blank for a moment. "Your bat . . ." she stammered. "I didn't know. Honest."

"See these notches? My father put them on."

"But they were covered up with tape. I had no idea it was yours." She looked at Jessie for support. "Why would I take someone's bat?"

"Where did you get the bat?" Jessie said.

"In my locker. I thought the coach put it there for me." Her eyes were welling up with tears. "My mother bought me a brand-new bat but I left it at home today. I'd never take something that wasn't mine." She wiped her arm across her eyes and hurried across the field.

"Well, now what?" Nicole asked. "Are you going to tell Coach Warren?"

"I'm just glad I got my bat back," Ann said. "I'm not going to say anything."

Chuck blew the whistle just then, and everyone returned to practice. Chuck was helping Jessie practice catching fly balls, when he spotted her autographed glove. "It says Hank Aaron. Is this for real?" He examined the signature. "I guess it is." He slipped his hand inside the glove. "I've always been a fan of his."

When they broke for lunch, Jessie put her glove in her locker. Mr. Jackson had assigned each player a green metal locker. Henry and Violet joined her at the picnic table, and Benny came racing up with Michael and Nicole. Everyone was starving.

In between bites of her cheese and tomato sandwich, Nicole told everyone about Susan and the bat.

"At least she got her bat back," Violet said.

"But it doesn't solve the mystery of who took it," Henry said. "Not if Susan's telling the truth."

"I'm sure she is," Nicole said. "She was really upset. She was crying!"

"Well, let's all be extra careful." Henry advised. "Jessie, where's your glove?" he said suddenly.

"It's safe," she told him. "Put away in my locker."

Except Jessie was in for a surprise. When she returned to her locker after lunch, she saw the door swinging open.

"Ohmigosh!" Nicole blurted out. "Someone's been in your locker. Is everything okay?"

Jessie looked inside. The locker was empty. "No, it's not okay," she said, close to tears. "My glove's gone."

Violet came up behind her just then, and realized what had happened. "Oh, Jessie, I'm so sorry," she said. "What do we do now?"

Henry, who was right behind Violet, spoke first. His voice was low, his expression tight. "We catch a thief," he said grimly.

CHAPTER 4

A Fake!

"I'm sure your glove will turn up, Jessie," Violet said the next day. "After all, Ann found her bat, didn't she?"

In the hands of another player, Jessie thought. It was nine o'clock in the morning, and everyone was lined up to practice hitting.

"Be more aggressive, Susan," Chuck shouted. The blonde girl nodded and hit the ball again as Jessie watched. After a few more hits, Chuck signaled for the next player to step forward, and Susan dropped back to the end of the line.

"I think we're getting better," she said to Jessie. "At first I couldn't hit the ball at all. Now I'm getting two out of three."

"All our practice is paying off," Jessie said.

"Baseball is taking up a lot of my time," Susan said. She flexed the fingers on her right hand. They were cramped from gripping the bat too tightly. "I've had to let my painting and drawing slide."

"You're an artist?"

Susan looked a little shy. "My aunt's the real artist in the family. She gives me art lessons every week, but I've had to cut back since I started coming here."

The line moved forward then, and Violet tried gripping the bat the way Chuck had showed her: fingers half an inch away from the knob, with the middle knuckles lined up.

Meanwhile, Benny was getting some advice on baseball from Mr. Jackson. "Do you know how to tell if you've got the right bat, Benny?" The two were sorting through the equipment during the morning's practice.

Benny shook his head. "No, they all look alike to me." He put down a stack of helmets, hoping Mr. Jackson would go on talking. There was so much he could learn about baseball, and he didn't want to miss a word.

"I'll show you a little trick, son," Mr. Jackson said, handing Benny a shiny new bat. He positioned Benny's arm so Benny was holding the bat straight out in front of him. "Count to ten, Benny."

"One . . . two . . . three . . ." Benny had no idea what Mr. Jackson was up to.

"Getting a bit tired?" The bat sagged a little as Benny kept on counting. "That means it's too heavy for you. The secret is to hold the bat straight out for ten seconds. If your arm doesn't droop, it means it's the right weight." He handed Benny another bat. "Try this one."

"Wow! I bet you know everything in the world about baseball."

"I've been around the game a long time," Mr. Jackson said. "Seen a lot of changes in my day." He paused and rubbed his neck thoughtfully. "Of course, not all the changes are for the good."

"Like what?" Benny scooted up onto a

workbench, with his feet dangling off the edge.

"In my day, baseball was a boy's game," Mr. Jackson said gruffly. "Nowadays the girls all play." He swept a screwdriver and a saltshaker off the workbench into a drawer.

Benny started to reply, but Henry walked into the dugout just then with a pile of clean towels. What was wrong with girls playing baseball? he wondered. His sisters played!

Later that morning, Nicole and Violet decided to dash to a nearby store for lemonade. Although the day was sunny and warm, the field had been muddy and practice had been hard. "We have ten minutes for break," Nicole said a little breathlessly. "That's three minutes each way, and four minutes to buy the drinks." Coach Warren was very strict about breaks, and anyone who came back late had to run laps.

"Is it lunchtime?" a dark-haired woman asked when they entered the store. Violet recognized her from tryouts. She had been with Susan Miller.

"Not yet," Violet said politely. "We just

have a short break. Are you Mrs. Miller?"

"No, I'm Susan's aunt, Edna Sealy," Mrs. Sealy said.

"It seems like I've been waiting for hours." She looked disgusted. "How long can that stupid game go on?"

Nicole and Violet exchanged a look. Mrs. Sealy didn't seem to like baseball. So why did she bother coming to practice?

"Did you see Susan hitting this morning?" Violet asked. "She's doing much better. Chuck says she has a lot of talent."

"I guess you could call it that," Mrs. Sealy said sourly. "If you think it takes any talent to hit a ball with a stick. And no, I didn't see her play. I dropped her off this morning and have been doing errands ever since." She watched as the girls scooped up their drinks. "Tell Susan to try to finish early." She sighed. "I'd like her to get some painting in today." She walked to the window, and Violet noticed that her tennis shoes were caked with bright red mud. Where had she seen that strange color before? she wondered.

"We will," Nicole said, darting out the

door. Poor Susan, she thought. The coach had already told them that practice would be running late. Her aunt would really be upset.

The Aldens had lunch with their new friends, Nicole and Michael.

"I don't think I'll ever be a pitcher," Michael moaned. "My arm feels like it's ready to drop off." He rubbed his upper arm with the flat of his hand.

"I know what you mean," Violet said sympathetically. "I've got some sore spots, too. Chuck said that we'll get used to it."

She opened a bag of sandwiches and passed the first one to Benny, who looked like he was starving. "Oh, we forgot the apples."

"I'll go get them," Jessie said, scrambling to her feet. "They're in my locker."

She hurried back to the lockers, and smiled at Mr. Jackson, who frowned at her. "I forgot something," she explained, as she flung open the locker door. She reached in without looking and was startled when her hand touched something leathery. "What in the world — " she began. It was her glove!

Grabbing the glove and clutching it to her chest, she ran all the way back to the picnic table.

"You found your glove!" Violet cried.

"Someone returned it," Jessie said happily. She felt so relieved! It wasn't until she sat down and took a closer look at the glove that she gasped out loud. "Wait a minute," she said slowly, "this isn't my glove. It's a *fake*!"

"How do you know?" Henry said quickly. He reached for the glove and turned it over, examining the signature.

"Look at the handwriting," Jessie said in a quavery voice. She felt close to tears. "Someone tried to forge the signature." She shook her head angrily. "They didn't do a very good job."

"You're right," Henry said finally. "It does look different."

"And the color's wrong," Benny piped up.

"That's true," Jessie agreed. "My glove was a little lighter. It was faded from being in the sunlight."

"So somebody went to a lot of trouble to

make you think you got your glove back," Michael said. "But who?"

"And why?" Nicole added.

"Whoever stole it. I guess they wanted to cover up the theft," Jessie suggested.

"This makes two thefts in less than a week," Henry pointed out. "I think we're going to have to keep our eyes open."

"How did somebody sneak this into Jessie's locker?" Benny asked.

"I don't know," Henry said slowly. "Think hard, Benny. Was there anyone hanging around the dugout besides you and Mr. Jackson? It must have happened sometime this morning."

"That's right," Jessie agreed. "My locker was empty when I put the apples in at eight o'clock."

Benny scrunched his face in thought and finally shook his head. "Nobody. I didn't see anybody in the dugout." He paused. "Except for Chuck."

"Chuck wouldn't take the glove," Nicole said quickly. She liked the friendly young man who was giving them so much help.

"I don't think so either, but . . . he admired it," Jessie said. "He told me Hank Aaron was his favorite player."

Violet turned the glove over in her hand. It had a rough, grainy texture, and the leather was coarsened. She saw tiny white specks caught in one of the seams. "That's funny," she said. "This looks like salt."

"Salt?" Michael was interested. He reached for the glove and rubbed his fingers gently over the surface. "You're right. Someone rubbed salt into it, to break down the leather. You know, to make it look old."

"Salt!" Benny blurted out. He clapped his hand over his mouth.

Everyone stared at him. "What's wrong?"

Benny looked around nervously, and when he spoke his voice was hardly a whisper. "Mr. Jackson had a saltshaker on his workbench today. I saw him put it into the drawer just as Henry walked in."

Henry's face was serious. "Do you think he was trying to hide it?"

Benny shrugged. "I don't know. He didn't act that way."

"Well, of course he'd try to act casual," Nicole pointed out. "If he was really guilty, of course. He wouldn't want you to be suspicious."

"I wasn't," Benny admitted. "At least not then." He sat lost in thought. He just couldn't imagine that Mr. Jackson would steal Jessie's glove and then try to replace it with a fake one. Why would he do such a thing? Suddenly he remembered something. "Hey!" he said.

"What is it, Benny?" Henry asked.

"You know what?" Benny said, "Mr. Jackson doesn't think girls should play baseball!"

"What?" Jessie was outraged. "You're kidding!"

"No, it's the truth." Benny told them about his conversation with Mr. Jackson.

"How weird. Do you think *he* was kidding?" Violet asked. She had noticed that Mr. Jackson had never been too friendly to her, but she found it hard to believe he didn't want her on the team.

"I don't know," Benny said, his eyes solemn. "But does this have anything to do with stealing Jessie's glove?"

Henry took a deep breath. "Maybe. If he really wants the girls off the team, I suppose he could make things hard for them, one by one. First Ann, and her missing bat, and then Jessie, and the missing glove."

"Maybe he thinks if he causes enough problems for the girls, they'll all quit," Michael said.

Jessie was angry. "Then he doesn't know us. I'll play whether I get my glove back or not."

"We all will," Violet said encouragingly. "Anyway, Mr. Jackson might not even be the thief. It might be someone else."

"But who?" Benny asked.

Chuck blew his whistle for everyone to come back to the field. "I don't know. We'll have to think about it," Henry said.

Somehow they had to solve the mystery before anything else disappeared.

CHAPTER 5

The Bears

"Meet our new mascot," Benny said to Nicole and Michael the next morning. He proudly held up a battered teddy bear. Jessie had made the bear from old stockings back when they lived in the boxcar. "This is Stockings," Benny told them.

"Very nice," Nicole said, panting a little. She squinted a little against the bright sunlight. They were starting their morning practice by running laps around the playing field. "But why do we need a mascot?"

"To bring us luck," Benny said seriously.

"Baseball players always need something to give them good luck. Didn't you know that?"

"Sure," Michael said. He dropped back a little to keep pace with Benny. "Some players make sure they tie their shoelaces the same way before every game and eat the same thing for breakfast. They think it makes them play better."

Benny nodded. "That's why I brought Stockings. There won't be anything else missing around here. You'll see."

"Whatever you say, Benny," Michael said with a chuckle. "Are you going to carry him around all day?"

"I sure am!" Benny insisted. He hesitated. "Except for lunch. I'll have to put him down when I eat my sandwich."

After they finished their laps, Chuck and Benny laid a sheet of plastic on the ground so they could practice sliding into a base. The sheet of plastic was about four feet wide and twenty feet long. When it was wet, it became very slippery. It was just like zipping over a patch of ice.

Chuck explained that sliding was important because it helped you reach a base safely without getting tagged out by the baseman. And it was important to practice on the plastic so no one would get hurt. Everyone took their shoes off and Violet went first. She backed up a few feet and waited for Chuck to signal her to go. She felt a little nervous and wasn't sure she would do it right.

"Remember, Violet," he said, "it's just like falling."

"That's what I'm afraid of," she protested.

"But this is falling without getting hurt," Chuck pointed out. "Remember what I told you? If you do it right, you won't hurt yourself or the other players. Just relax and go with the fall."

"I'll try," Violet said.

"Go for it!" Susan Miller encouraged her.

"Keep your head up!" Henry yelled.

Violet took a deep breath and dashed toward the plastic strip. When her foot touched it, she immediately let herself go into a controlled fall, and tried to stay relaxed. It worked! Jessie applauded and Chuck gave her a thumbs-up sign.

All the players took turns on the plastic until Chuck was satisfied that everyone knew how to slide safely.

After lunch, Coach Warren called everyone together in the center of the field. "Listen up," he said. His face was ruddy from the sun and he tapped his clipboard. "I have a challenge for you. How'd you like to play a real game the day after tomorrow?"

"A real game?" Violet blurted out. To that point, they had just been practicing their skills. Chuck had gone over the rules of the game with them, but were they ready to take their positions on the baseball diamond?

"Do you mean it?" Benny asked excitedly. He was all set to root the team on to victory.

"Who would we be playing against?" Michael asked.

"Beginners, I hope," Nicole said under her breath.

"It's a team over in the next county, and they're starting out, just like you." Coach Warren looked down at his clipboard. "They call themselves the Pirates, and they've been playing for a month. Their coach called me

last night, and asked if we'd be interested."
He waited while everyone thought it over.
"Well," he said finally, "are you ready for
it?"

"We're ready!" Benny shouted. Everyone
laughed. Leave it to Benny to speak for the
whole team.

"Anybody else?" Coach Warren asked.

"I think we can do it," Henry volunteered.

"So do I," Michael spoke up.

"We might as well give it a try," Nicole
said with a shrug.

"Let's do it," Susan Miller said.

"Count me in," Jessie offered, stepping
forward.

"Me, too," Violet echoed. She was really
getting better, and was excited at the thought
of a real game.

Coach Warren grinned. "Great." He
glanced at his watch. "Let's get to work, because game time is just two days away. Ten
o'clock in Clarksville."

"So it's us against the Pirates," Henry said.

"Hey," Benny said suddenly, "what are
we called?"

"That's a good point," Chuck said. "We need to choose a name."

"We better find one quick." Jessie looked at her teammates. "Anyone have any ideas?"

Benny thought hard. Tigers, ducks, wildcats, bulls . . . what would be a good name? Then he remembered his mascot, Stockings. "I've got it," he yelled. He held up Stockings. "We can be the Bears."

"The Bears. I like it!" Susan patted him on the back. Everyone started cheering, until Coach Warren blew his whistle. "Okay, now that we've got that settled, let's get back to practice." He tugged on the peak of his baseball cap and looked at them very seriously. "Play ball, Bears!"

Later that afternoon, a little four-year-old girl appeared at the edge of the field. She was wearing a pink sundress, and holding Mr. Jackson's hand.

"This is my granddaughter," Mr. Jackson said proudly, when Jessie and Benny wandered over during a break. "Her name's Sarah."

"Hi, Sarah." Jessie bent down so she was

on eye level with the little girl. "That's a pretty doll you have." She pointed to a Raggedy Ann doll that Sarah was clutching.

"She loves dolls," Mr. Jackson said. "Stuffed animals, too. Her room's full of them."

Sarah stayed for the rest of the practice, watching as Jessie and Violet worked on their pitching and fielding.

"I'll never get these ground balls," Violet said. She shook her head as the third ball in a row skirted past her ankles.

"Remember what Henry said," Michael reminded her. "Hold your glove with the fingers to the ground. That way you can scoop up the ball as it rolls into the glove."

"And don't shut your eyes," Jessie reminded her.

"I'll try," Violet promised. This time she didn't turn her head or squeeze her eyes shut. She looked straight at the ball, dropped to one knee and scooped it up as it whizzed right into her glove. "I got it!" she said happily.

Before practice broke up, Coach Warren gathered everyone together for a little pep talk. The sun was setting and a soft breeze swept over the playing field. The Aldens were sitting cross-legged on the grass as the Coach paced up and down in front of the players.

"You've been working hard," he said, "and I think we've got a good team." He glanced at Henry and Benny. "And I don't mean just the players. Our two special assistants have done a great job." Benny looked at Henry and broke into a wide grin.

"But I want to give you a little advice." He clapped his hands behind his back and strode up and down. "Do you know the first rule of baseball?"

Susan called out. "Keep your eye on the ball?"

Coach Warren nodded. "That's part of it. I was thinking of the bigger picture." He paused and looked at the circle of players. "Something I've had to remind you of from time to time."

Nicole guessed it. "Keep your mind on the game?" Just yesterday, Chuck had caught her daydreaming while she was waiting for the pitcher to throw the ball.

"That's it," the coach said approvingly. "I want you to think about the game *all* the time."

"I think we do. Usually," Michael spoke up. He grinned. "But I guess we all can try harder."

"That's the spirit," Coach Warren said. "Remember, there may be innings when you have nothing to do in the outfield. Even if your body has nothing to do, keep your mind working. Watch every pitch and be ready. The hitter may send the ball right to you. Yell to your teammates to encourage them. Talk to them about the game . . . how many outs . . . who is at bat . . . who's backing up the players on the infield."

Violet scuffed her toe in the soft red earth. She knew the coach was right. Sometimes when she was waiting to take her turn at bat, she drifted off into a world of her own.

"Don't listen to the crowds," Coach Warren went on. "Don't talk to anyone but your teammates. Don't be thinking of anything but the ball game. Can you do that?"

"You bet we can!" Benny leaped to his feet and everyone joined him. "Nobody can stop the Bears!"

Coach Warren looked at Chuck. "I think we've got ourselves a team."

Half an hour later, the Aldens, along with Michael and Nicole, stopped at the grocery for a quick drink before heading home. It was very warm out, and Violet was longing for a lemonade.

"How do you feel about playing the Pirates?" Violet asked. Nicole acted very confident on the outside, but she suspected that her new friend was feeling as nervous as she was.

"A little scared," Nicole admitted. "I probably wouldn't say that to anyone but you, though."

"Me, too," Violet paid for the drinks and carried them back to the small table where the rest of the group was waiting. A few minutes later, they noticed Chuck buying a package of gum in the front of the store. He was with a boy about eleven years old, and didn't see the Aldens.

"Who's that with Chuck?" Nicole whispered.

"I don't know," Henry said.

After Chuck and the young boy had left, Benny patted his duffel bag. "Stockings brought us good luck today," he said proudly. "Nothing else missing, and we get to play another team."

"Just make sure you bring him the day after tomorrow," Violet said. "I'm going to need all the good luck I can get."

"So where is our mascot?" Nicole asked.

"Right here." Benny reached into his duffel bag. "I'll bring him out so he can join us." He groped inside the bag, and his expression suddenly became alarmed. "Oh no!" he wailed.

"What's wrong?" Violet said quickly.

Benny took everything out of the duffel bag and turned it inside out on the seat. There was no sign of the stuffed bear. "He's gone," Benny said hoarsely. "Stockings is gone!"

"Oh, no, Benny! Are you sure?" asked Jessie.

Benny frowned. "Yes," he said. "Someone *took* him!"

Nicole shook her head in dismay. A stolen bat, a stolen glove, and now the team mascot was missing. What did this mean for the Bears?

CHAPTER 6

A Long Way to Clarksville

"I'm so nervous I don't think I can hold onto the bat," Violet whispered to Nicole.

Nicole nodded. "My hands are slippery, too. And I feel like I swallowed a whole jar full of butterflies." She tugged the visor down on her cap. "Let's just hope the other team is as scared as we are."

It was eight in the morning and everyone was gathered at the playing field. Violet tried to ignore the fact that her stomach was growling. She had barely touched the hot oatmeal that Mrs. McGregor had prepared that morning. She had been too excited thinking about the game! Would she remember everything Chuck had told her? Would she score a run? Would the team be proud of her?

Benny was the only one who seemed calm. He had polished off two bowls of oatmeal and a double helping of French toast.

Now Henry stood next to his little brother and ruffled Benny's hair. "How's it going, Benny?"

"Okay, I guess." Benny scuffed his toe in the soft red earth. "I miss Stockings, though. And today's our very first game. We need him for luck!" Benny had checked the dugout that morning, hoping to find the stuffed bear.

"Maybe Stockings can still bring us luck," Violet said. "From wherever he is." She knew her little brother was disappointed. "After all, he's still our mascot, even if he's not with us."

Benny brightened. "That's right," he said. "I never thought of that."

"Let's hit the road, everybody!" Chuck blew his whistle and slid open the doors on

Coach Warren's navy blue van. All their equipment was packed in a metal container on the roof.

Violet, Jessie, and Nicole piled into the back of the van and Benny slid in next to them. Benny loved to ride in a car and hoped everyone would sing or play games once they got under way.

When all the players were settled and had fastened their seatbelts, Coach Warren turned the ignition key. Nothing happened. He frowned and tried again. "That's funny," he said. After a third time, he turned to Chuck. "It's dead. Completely dead."

Chuck glanced at the gas gauge. It was full. "Why don't you give it another try?"

After a few more minutes, Coach Warren swiveled around in his seat. "I'm afraid we've got a problem, gang. This van isn't going anywhere." When everyone groaned, he held up his hand. "Don't worry, all we need to do is switch vans. Just give me a minute and I'll get the keys to the red one. It's a little smaller, but at least it'll get us there." When he disappeared into the office, Benny sighed.

"You don't think this happened because Stockings is missing, do you? Maybe we're in for a string of bad luck."

"Of course we're not," Violet reassured him. "Everything is going to be fine. We'll switch vans and we'll be on the road in a few minutes. You'll see."

Except it wasn't that simple. When Coach Warren reappeared a few minutes later, his face was red. "I can't understand it," he said, when Chuck hopped out of the blue van to meet him. "I can't find the keys."

"They're on the hook by the door," Benny said. He had noticed that the coach always kept them there.

"Not this time," Coach Warren said. He thought for a moment. "When's the last time you saw them there, Benny?"

Benny shrugged. "Maybe yesterday or the day before. But not today."

"That's what I was afraid of." Coach Warren scratched his head. "I don't understand what could have happened to them."

"Have you checked your pockets?" Henry asked.

The coach turned his pockets inside out but there was no sign of the missing keys. He turned to Chuck. "Did you happen to notice them this morning?"

"I haven't been in the office," Chuck said.

Wait a minute — that's not true, Jessie thought silently. She had noticed Chuck coming out of the office when she crossed the field. Had he forgotten? Or was he lying? She closed her eyes and tried to remember exactly what she had seen. Yes, she decided. The sun had been in her eyes, but she had seen Chuck walking out of the office with someone right behind him. Who was it? Suddenly the figure came into focus in her mind. It was Mr. Jackson. Both of them had been in the office. Could one of them have taken the keys? But why?

"We'll have to find those keys," the coach muttered. "And if they don't turn up, we'll have to get this van started."

When Chuck and Coach Warren went back into the office to search again for the keys, Henry opened the hood on the van.

"What are we looking for?" Nicole asked,

peering at the engine. "I wonder if the van needs oil . . ." Henry suddenly gasped. "Look at this!" he pointed to a jagged set of cables. Someone had sliced right through them!

"What is it?" Michael and Jessie hurried over.

"Someone's cut the cables to the battery," Henry explained. "No wonder the engine wouldn't start."

"But who would do something like that?" Violet was shocked. She couldn't believe that anyone would really want to hurt the team. The thefts were one thing, but now a whole game was at stake!

Henry showed Chuck and Coach Warren what he had discovered. "It's hard to believe," the coach said as he stood peering at the jagged ends of battery cable.

"I guess there's no way it could have happened accidentally?" Jessie said softly.

"I'm afraid not." Chuck shook his head.

"Looks like someone doesn't want us to get to Clarksville," Coach Warren remarked.

"Could it be someone on the Pirates team?" Michael asked.

"No chance of that." The coach took off his baseball cap and wiped his brow. "I talked to Coach Evert last night, and they can't wait to beat the pants off us." He smiled grimly. "They're already planning a victory pizza party for after the game."

Benny was angry. "How do they know they're going to win? We've got the best team around!"

"I think so, too, Benny," Coach Warren said. "But we can't prove it if we can't get to the game."

"How about your pickup truck, Chuck," the coach said suddenly.

"My truck?" Chuck looked doubtful. He glanced at the truck parked at the edge of the field. But then he brightened. "All right. We can't miss our first game."

Coach Warren slapped Chuck on the back. "Okay, team, let's a get a move on. We've got a game to play!"

Henry helped Chuck unload the equipment from the van and hand it to the players. "Two people can sit up front with me," Chuck announced, "and everyone else can pile in the back. There's a couple of blankets back there. Spread them on the bed of the truck so you don't get dirty."

Within minutes the truck was loaded, and Susan was wedged in between Jessie and Violet in the back of the truck. "Aren't you coming with us, Coach?" Jessie asked in surprise.

"I want to wait around for the road service. I called them when the van wouldn't start. Don't worry," he added. "Chuck will take good care of you, and I'll get to Clarksville in plenty of time."

Chuck made a thumbs-up gesture and pulled smoothly out onto the highway. "This is fun," Benny said, leaning against Violet. It was a warm day, and he loved to ride in the open air.

"Anybody hungry?" Susan asked. "Besides you, Benny," she added, and everyone laughed. She opened a large plastic bag of brownies and passed it around.

"These are great," Violet said, biting into

one. "Where did they come from?"

"My aunt made them," Susan replied. "She dropped them off before we started loading the van."

They had been driving for over half an hour, when Chuck suddenly pulled to the side of the road.

"What's wrong?" Nicole asked. Henry slid out of the front seat. "Chuck just wants to study the map," he explained.

"You mean we're lost?" Benny wailed. "I knew it. It's all because Stockings is missing."

"We're not lost, Benny," Chuck said. He spread open the map on the hood of the truck. "I just need to get my bearings."

"Where are we?" Nicole asked. They were on a dusty country road, bounded by farmland. In a nearby field, a group of black and white cows stared at them curiously.

"I don't know for sure," Chuck admitted.

"That means we're lost," Benny whispered.

"Do you know if we're even on the right road to Clarksville?" Violet asked. She was already nervous about the upcoming game, and it seemed like they were in the middle of one disaster after another!

"Not really," Chuck admitted.

"Maybe Coach Warren is already there," Michael said. "Maybe he's wondering where we are."

Chuck groaned. "I hope not." He held the map up and stared at a rusty road sign. "Route seven," he said, shaking his head. "That's not even on the map."

"Could we retrace our steps?" Henry suggested. "I think we left the main highway about ten minutes ago. Remember when we passed the fruit stand? We could go back there and get directions."

"Good idea," Chuck agreed. "I just hope we can find it."

They piled back into the truck, and Jessie glanced at her watch. They had been on the road for forty-five minutes and Chuck didn't even know where they were! And now they were heading for a fruit stand that might be impossible to find. How could so many things go wrong?

She looked at Benny, who had his eyes tightly closed. "What's wrong?" she whispered.

"I'm sending a secret message to Stockings wherever he is," Benny said softly. "We need a mascot right *now*."

Nicole overheard the conversation and smiled. "Tell Stockings we're counting on him," she said. She shifted her weight as the truck bounced along the bumpy road. "Because I've got the feeling that it's going to be a long, long way to Clarksville!"

CHAPTER 7

Play Ball!

"Just play your best," Coach Warren said an hour later as the team huddled around him. "That's all anybody expects of you." The van had been fixed and he'd made it to Clarksville before the others.

Chuck had gotten lost three more times, but the Bears had finally arrived, and the big game was about to begin. Everyone's nerves were on edge.

"And be a good sport, whether you win or lose," Chuck added. Jessie nodded, but she was beginning to wonder if the game was doomed from the start. So many things had gone wrong! She nervously checked out the opposing team. They all looked so confident! A girl close to her own age was taking practice swings with her bat, and the pitcher was throwing pitches to the catcher.

"They look pretty good, don't they?" Nicole said under her breath. She didn't want to admit it, but she was feeling a little nervous. Would doing her best be good enough?

Coach Warren had assigned their positions at the last practice. Jessie was at first base, Ann at second, and Michael at third. Susan was playing shortstop. A boy named Tom was pitching and his brother Steve was catching. Nicole and Violet were in the outfield with a boy named Bobby.

The Pirates were batting first, so the Bears ran to take their places on the field.

Once the game got under way, Violet felt some of her nervousness vanish. The Bears played well, and soon it was their turn to bat. When Violet came up to bat, she was thrilled to hear a satisfying *crack* as the bat hit the ball. Henry had told her that there

was no other sound in the world quite like it, and he was right!

Violet watched as the ball flew out toward center field, and she raced around the bases. Rounding first base she saw Coach Warren waving her on. She headed to second base and saw that the center fielder hadn't caught the ball, so she ran hard to third base. As she reached third she saw that the center fielder had thrown to second base, and the second baseman had dropped the ball. Violet took a deep breath and ran as hard as she could. As she tagged home plate she heard her teammates cheering. She'd hit a home run!

Jessie's big moment at first base came late in the game. The Pirate batter hit a hard grounder along the first base line. Jessie charged into action. She snatched up the ball and stepped on first base just before the runner.

"Way to go, Jessie!" Chuck yelled from the sidelines. She looked over and saw him give her the thumbs-up sign. I did it! she thought happily. Suddenly what Coach

Warren said earlier made sense. It didn't really matter if the Bears won or lost. All she had to do was do her best!

As the game went on, it was obvious that the Pirates had more experience than the Bears, and had practiced a lot. The Bears managed to keep up at first, but in the last inning the Pirates scored two runs to win the game.

The final score was Bears 5, Pirates 7. The two coaches shook hands, and the Bears headed toward the van.

"You mean that's it? It's over?" Benny said. He looked sad.

"Don't worry, Benny," Henry said. "We can always play them again." He took a long swig of water from Benny's bottle.

"I wanted us to win *now*," Benny said. He immediately thought of Stockings. He knew everything would have turned out differently if his mascot had been with them.

"You should feel good about yourselves," Coach Warren said as they piled into the van. "You did a great job, especially for your first real game."

"I made a ton of mistakes," Jessie said.

"Me too," said Nicole.

"That's okay. A good player learns from her mistakes. She practices harder to keep from making the same mistakes again. And that's what I expect you to do."

"I think he just said that to make us feel better," Nicole said to Chuck when Coach Warren moved away.

"No, he really means it," Chuck said seriously. "We all make mistakes, and hey, what would baseball be without errors and strikeouts?"

"Even big-name players strike out," Henry pointed out. "Nobody's perfect."

The next morning, the Aldens arrived at the dugout early, and Benny headed for the locker room. He was surprised to see Mr. Jackson fumbling with the combination lock on his locker.

"Oh, hello, Benny," Mr. Jackson said nervously, smoothing his gray hair. "I didn't hear you come in." He quickly moved away from the locker and wiped his hands on his overalls.

"What are you doing?" Benny asked curiously.

"Just checking the lockers," Mr. Jackson answered. He tried to smile, but his voice was tense.

"What for?" Benny persisted.

Mr. Jackson avoided looking at him. "Well, I . . . I'm thinking of repainting them," he stammered. "The paint's getting pretty chipped in spots, you know."

Benny looked at the gleaming row of bright green lockers and frowned. Chuck had told him that the lockers had been freshly painted a few months ago! Was Mr. Jackson lying to him? Was he really trying to break into his locker?

Later that morning, Jessie stopped to refill her water bottle and saw Mr. Jackson deep in conversation with Mrs. Sealy.

"I can't wait to see the look on Coach Warren's face," Mr. Jackson said.

"Neither can I," Mrs. Sealy agreed. "He's going to be in for the shock of his life."

Chuck blew his whistle just then, signaling the end of break time, and Jessie returned to the playing field. Were Mr. Jackson and Mrs. Sealy plotting something? Mrs. Sealy called it "the shock of his life." Were they going to do something that would embarrass Coach Warren? Surely neither one of them would have any reason to sabotage the team, would they? But what was the big secret? Jessie thought about it all morning, and couldn't come up with any answers.

It wasn't until they were eating lunch at the long picnic table that Nicole nudged her. "What's wrong?" she asked. "You're so quiet!"

Jessie hesitated. Was this the right time to bring up what was really bothering her? She glanced around the table. Only Nicole and Michael had joined the Aldens for lunch. The others had preferred to sit under the shade of a giant elm tree. Maybe if they all put their heads together, they could come up with an explanation.

"I think we need to clear the air," she said softly, and everyone turned to look at her. "There've been some strange things going on lately . . ." she began.

"I'll say," Benny interrupted her. "Someone's been going around stealing teddy bears!" He missed Stockings and continued to look for him every day.

"I know, Benny," she said sympathetically, "but I'm talking about more than just teddy bears."

"Weird things have been happening right from the start," Henry spoke up. "Remember when Ann's bat was missing and ended up in Susan's locker?"

"And that was just the beginning," Violet said. "Jessie's glove was taken, and someone tried to trick her with a phony one."

"I never did get back my glove," Jessie said.

"I think it will turn up." Nicole gently squeezed her friend's arm.

"Yeah, maybe the same person who took your glove took Stockings," Benny piped up. "Maybe they'll feel so bad about taking them, that they'll return them both."

"And we nearly missed the game with the Pirates yesterday because so many things went wrong." Michael looked serious. "First someone cut the cables to the van, and then the keys were missing."

"Plus Chuck got lost a lot out in the country," Violet reminded him. "I'm surprised we made it there in time."

"Do you think it's just a string of coincidences?" Nicole asked. She took a bite of her sandwich. It seemed hard to believe that someone would really want to sabotage the team.

"I think it's more than that," Henry said. "So many things have happened that it seems like more than just a run of bad luck."

"Something else happened at the game," Michael said suddenly. "I didn't think of it before, but did anyone notice number thirty-eight on the Pirates team? A short kid with sandy hair?"

"I think I did," Benny said. "What about him?"

"I've seen him before." Michael paused and looked around the table. "All of us have. He was buying a soft drink with Chuck the other day in the store."

"That's right!" Violet burst out. "I knew he looked familiar!"

"But what does that mean?" Jessie asked. "Do you think Chuck is involved somehow in everything that's gone wrong?"

"I hate to think so," Henry told her.

Jessie nodded. "He said he hadn't been in the office when the keys were missing, but he was lying. I saw him walk out of the office a few minutes earlier, and Mr. Jackson was with him."

"Wow," Benny said softly. "Mr. Jackson might be involved, too."

"Why do you say that, Benny?" Henry asked.

Benny told them about Mr. Jackson snooping around his locker that morning.

"There's something else you don't know," Jessie said. "I heard a really strange conversation between Mr. Jackson and Mrs. Sealy this morning. It sounded like they were planning a surprise for Coach Warren — but not the kind of surprise you'd look forward to," she said grimly.

"Mrs. Sealy said she hates baseball, but she's always around," Nicole pointed out.

Violet frowned. "A lot of things about her don't make sense." Suddenly she remembered something else. "Remember when we saw her in the store that day and she said she hadn't been on the playing field? She wasn't telling us the truth! I *know* she'd been over here. She had red mud all over her shoes."

"You know, she must have been here when the van keys were missing, too," Nicole added.

"How do you know that?" Michael asked.

Nicole leaned forward eagerly. "Because Susan passed around a bag of brownies in the truck. She said her aunt had dropped them off for us that morning."

"That's right!" Jessie said. "So now we have three suspects, Chuck, Mrs. Sealy, and Mr. Jackson." She paused. "But I still can't figure out why any one of them would want to hurt the team."

"Mr. Jackson doesn't think girls should play baseball," Benny piped up.

"And Mrs. Sealy thinks Susan is wasting her time playing with us," Nicole offered. "She thinks she could be painting pictures."

"What about Chuck?" Benny asked.

Henry shrugged. "Maybe Chuck is secretly rooting for the other team because he has a friend — that little boy — who plays for them."

There was a long silence. "I think we have a long way to go before we solve this mystery," Jessie said.

"You're right," Violet told her. "But let's do it before anything else gets stolen."

CHAPTER 8

Henry Has an Idea

On Saturday morning, the Aldens trooped into the kitchen for an early breakfast. "I made waffles," Mrs. McGregor said as they settled around the oak table. "I know you want to get an early start for the fairgrounds." It was the day of the annual Greenfield flea market, and the children had invited Michael and Nicole to join them.

"What's a flea market, anyway?" Benny asked, pouring a tall glass of orange juice.

"It's like a giant yard sale," Jessie told him.

"People come from all over town and set up booths to sell things."

"What kind of things?"

"Just about everything. Furniture and dolls and antiques . . ."

"Oh." Benny looked disappointed.

"Cheer up, Benny," Violet said teasingly. "There will be lots of good things to eat, like homemade cookies and cakes and dough-nuts."

"Oh, *good*!" Benny said, polishing off a waffle and reaching for another. "Then I know I'll like it."

Half an hour later, they met Michael and Nicole and headed for the fairgrounds. "This is going to be fun," Nicole said. "I can hardly wait to get there."

"And guess what," Michael spoke up. "Did you see the notice in today's paper? Someone's selling baseball cards and auto-graphs!"

"Let's head there first," Henry said.

The fairgrounds were crowded when the children arrived. Everyone was excited by a display of gingerbread houses. "Oh, they're pretty," Nicole said. "They look just like something out of Hansel and Gretel."

"But I bet they're really expensive," Violet said. She had brought her allowance money with her in case she wanted to buy something.

"Maybe we can learn to make them ourselves," Jessie suggested. The Aldens always loved to figure out how to do things on their own.

Benny asked the woman behind the booth, "Can you eat the houses?"

She laughed. "I certainly hope not. Each one of them took almost a whole week to decorate."

"C'mon," Henry said, putting his arm around his younger brother's shoulders. "Let's take a look at those baseball cards."

A large group was gathered around the baseball card vendor's booth, and Michael recognized a familiar face. "See that woman in the red dress?" he whispered to the others. "Isn't that Susan's aunt — the one who's always hanging around the field?"

Nicole watched as a dark-haired woman

backed out of the crowd and headed toward another booth. "That's her, all right. I wonder what she was doing at this booth?"

"It can't be because she likes baseball," Jessie said. "She thinks it's a waste of time."

"Well, I think it's the most fun game in the whole world," Benny said loudly.

"You're right," Henry said, laughing. "Now let's see the cards for ourselves."

They had been sorting through bins of cards for a few minutes when Benny suddenly grabbed Jessie's arm. "That's it!" he said hoarsely.

"That's what?" Jessie said blankly. She was looking at a baseball card that pictured Hank Aaron and listed his 733 home runs.

"Your glove!" Benny said, continuing to tug at her. "The one Aunt Jane gave you."

"What — where?" Now he had her full attention.

Benny pointed silently to a slightly battered glove just out of reach on a display shelf. The autograph was clearly visible — Hank Aaron.

"Can I see that glove — the one on the

left?" Jessie asked the man running the booth. She was so excited her hands were trembling. How in the world had her glove ended up here? Had someone stolen it from the dugout and sold it?

"This is a nice glove. I can give you a good price on it."

Jessie turned it over thoughtfully in her hands. It certainly looked like her glove! But she wasn't sure what to say. She couldn't accuse the man of stealing it! "I . . . I had a glove just like this one," she said finally. "My aunt gave it to me."

"You mean you had a glove signed by Hank Aaron," the man said in a friendly voice.

"That's right!" Jessie said.

"So do lots of people," he replied, arranging a stack of baseball caps.

Jessie was puzzled. "What do you mean?"

"The big-name players sign lots of gloves. Everybody knows that."

"I didn't," Jessie said softly. She slipped her hand inside the glove. There was a little rough spot inside that rubbed against her

knuckle — just like her glove. Was it hers? And anyway what could she do? Even if it was, there was no way she could prove it.

"How much is it?" Henry asked. He had seen the look on his sister's face, and he was determined to buy the glove for her.

But when the man told them the price, it was very high.

"Oh, no," Violet said softly. "Mine was stolen." She knew there was no way they could afford that. "Maybe if we all saved for it," she began doubtfully.

"You say you had a glove that was stolen?" the man asked Jessie. When she nodded, he went on, "That's really a shame. Tell you what I can do. I'll set this one aside until you've earned the money."

"Really?" Jessie asked, her face lighting up. "Thank you."

Later that afternoon, the children visited a booth filled with beautiful leather belts and handbags. Violet ran her hand over a tan belt, so soft it felt almost buttery. A young girl with a ponytail sitting on a stool said proudly, "I made that one myself."

"It's so pretty," Violet said. "Look, Benny, it has a cowboy design carved into it."

Benny touched the belt. "It's nice. How did you get it so smooth?"

"I have a secret ingredient," the girl told him smilingly. She reached for a saltshaker on the countertop. "Salt."

"Salt?" Violet and Benny said together.

The girl nodded and stood up. "When you want to soften leather, you soak it for awhile and then rub salt into it. Instead of being hard and stiff, it makes the leather soft, as if you've been wearing the belt for awhile."

Benny stood silently for a moment, thinking. That was what Michael had said when they'd found traces of salt on Jessie's glove — the fake one that someone had put in her locker. And Mr. Jackson always kept a saltshaker in the dugout. Was he the guilty one?

Toward the end of the day, the children ate hot dogs in the shade.

"Do you think that was really your glove?" Nicole asked her.

Jessie shrugged. "I'm not sure. It certainly looked like it and felt like it."

"But that still doesn't explain how it got here," Violet pointed out.

"We're never going to figure that part out," Michael said. "At least not until we catch the thief." He sipped some apple juice through a straw.

"I've been thinking about that." Henry leaned forward. "Maybe we shouldn't just sit back and wait for the thief to strike again."

"But what can we do?" Violet asked. "We can't catch him until he commits another crime."

Henry snapped his fingers. "That's it, exactly. And you know what? We can set him up so he *has* to commit another crime. He just won't be able to resist."

Michael looked interested. "You mean we offer him something, and once he grabs it — "

"We grab him!" Nicole finished for him.

"A trap!" Henry said. "You've got it." He looked at the other children. "So what do you think?"

"What could we offer him?" Jessie asked. "It would have to be something he'd really like to have."

"He already has my teddy bear," Benny said sadly.

Jessie put her arm around him. "I have a feeling we'll get Stockings back for you, Benny, even though I can't promise." She paused. "I think we have to offer him something to do with baseball. After all, look what he's stolen — a bat, a glove, and a mascot."

"And there's more than that going on," Nicole pointed out. "He took the keys to the van, cut the battery cables, and almost made us miss our game with the Pirates."

"You keep saying 'he,'" Michael reminded her. "We don't know that for sure. It could be a she."

"That's true," Violet agreed. "But there's one thing we're sure of. Everything is somehow connected to baseball."

"And that's exactly the way we trap him or her," Henry said. "We offer the thief some kind of baseball trophy, or autograph. Something that he just can't pass up."

"I know," said Jessie. "Something we saw back there." She jerked her thumb toward the row of booths.

"What's that?" Benny asked.

Jessie smiled. "Something small, something easy to hide, something easy to steal. And something the thief would really like to have if he likes baseball."

Benny scrunched his forehead. What was Jessie getting at? "I got it!" he said suddenly. "A baseball card. We're going to catch him with a baseball card."

"You're right, Benny," Jessie said eagerly. She scrambled to her feet and threw her napkin in the trash. "Who wants to help me pick one out?"

"I do," Benny said, jumping up. He was happy they had a plan. He could hardly wait to catch the thief. Whoever stole the glove and the bat had taken Stockings. Benny was sure of that. And when Benny caught up with him — or her — there would be a lot of explaining to do!

CHAPTER 9

Setting a Trap

Half an hour later, they had made their choice. Benny picked out a baseball card with a picture of a famous player, Joe DiMaggio.

"I hope the thief falls for this," he whispered as Henry paid for the card.

"He will if we lay our trap carefully." Henry tucked the card into his jacket pocket.

"What are we going to do exactly?" Nicole asked. They moved away from the booth. She and Jessie were sharing a lemon ice, and it was melting quickly in the hot sun.

"We're going to pretend this is a birthday present for Coach Warren," Henry explained. "A *surprise* birthday present."

"And we'll make sure everyone on the team knows about the card," Jessie said, her face lighting up. "Then the thief will have a chance to steal it."

"We'll hide it someplace really obvious," Henry continued.

"And when the thief shows up, we'll be waiting," Violet finished.

"So he'll be the one who's in for a surprise!" Benny said.

"You said everyone on the *team* will know," Nicole pointed out. "What about Chuck?"

"We'll make sure he knows, too," Henry promised.

"I bet someone will come forward," Nicole offered.

Henry patted his pocket. "I think so, too. This card will lure them."

The Aldens spent a quiet Sunday with Grandfather, and returned to practice early on Monday morning. They were scheduled to play the Pirates the very next day.

"Remember to catch the ball with *two* hands, Violet," Chuck shouted as he crossed the field. "And Jessie, let's see some power when you swing the bat!"

Henry was hitting fly balls to Nicole. Chuck stood watching them for a few minutes. "That's much better, Nicole," he said.

"I've really been working hard on it," she answered. She knew she didn't dare take her eyes off the ball. Henry hit one to her again, and she made a perfect catch. She brushed her hair out of her eyes and grinned when Chuck applauded.

"Nice work, Nicole!"

"Thanks!" She knew she had played well, and she felt good.

As the day passed, the Aldens spread the word to everyone about the present they had bought for Coach Warren.

"It's a surprise," Benny said to Susan Miller at lunchtime, putting his finger over his lips.

"Don't worry, Benny," she told him. "I can keep a secret."

"Joe DiMaggio," Violet mouthed to Ann in the middle of practice as the two girls waited their turn at bat. Ann looked impressed.

"Don't drag your right foot, Jessie!" Coach Warren yelled. "Remember to plant it."

Ann waited until Jessie hit the ball with a sharp crack, and whispered back, "He's going to love it. When are you going to give it to him?"

"Right after tomorrow's game."

"I hope it's someplace safe," Ann said.

"It is," Violet assured her. "It's in the glove compartment of the van . . ."

Late that afternoon, the Aldens gathered on Grandfather's front porch with Michael and Nicole. Mrs. McGregor had made lemonade for everyone, and Benny was dangling his legs off the porch swing.

"How do you feel about tomorrow?" Michael asked Violet. "Any butterflies?"

Violet shook her head. "Not yet. I may get a few tomorrow morning though, when

we get to the field." She rubbed her arm. It was tired from throwing. "Right now, I can't even think about playing a single inning."

"I feel the same way," Jessie said. "I can't worry about the game right now. I'm still thinking about the baseball card that Henry planted in the glove compartment."

"You mean you're wondering who's going to steal it," Nicole offered.

Jessie nodded. "It's so hard to believe that the thief is someone on the team."

"It's even harder to believe that it could be Chuck," Violet said. She liked the friendly young man who had tried so hard to help her with her throwing. "I still can't figure out why he would want to hurt the Bears."

"We saw him with one of the Pirates team members in the store that day," Henry reminded her.

"That's true," Violet admitted.

"And he said that Hank Aaron was one of his favorite players," Michael suggested. "So he'd have a good reason for taking Jessie's glove."

"A lot of people would like to have that glove," Henry said. He looked at Benny. "Has Mr. Jackson ever said anything that sounded suspicious to you?"

Benny shook his head. "Just that he doesn't think girls should play baseball."

Nicole, Violet, and Jessie groaned. "There's something else funny about him," Benny said. "Remember the saltshaker on his workbench? He might have used that to make the new glove look old."

Everyone was quiet for a moment, lost in thought.

"He was fooling around with the lockers, too," Benny added. "He said that he was thinking of painting them, but they don't need it. Honest!"

"Why would he lie?" Violet asked softly.

"Unless he has something to hide," Jessie answered.

"Mrs. Sealy doesn't tell the truth either," Violet pointed out. "Remember that day we saw her in the store? She said she hadn't been to the dugout, but I don't think that's true. She had red mud all over her shoes."

"And she was on the field the day someone cut the cables on the van," Henry pointed out. "She brought brownies for Susan to pass around."

Benny nodded. "I remember them. They were good!"

Violet laughed and tousled her brother's hair. "You would remember something like that!"

"It sounded like she was plotting something with Mr. Jackson," Jessie said. "Remember when she said that the coach was going to get the 'surprise of his life'?"

"Well, there's nothing we can do but wait until tomorrow," Henry said. He leaned back in the white wicker chair. "If everything goes the way I think it will, we'll have our thief."

CHAPTER 10

Plenty of Surprises

"I think we have a shot at it," Jessie whispered to Violet the next day. "I think we can actually beat them!" They were playing against the Pirates on their own turf, and the Bears were in the lead.

Violet nodded, a little dazed. She couldn't believe how well everyone on the team was playing! She had surprised herself and made some good hits. All the long hours of practice had paid off, just as Chuck had said they would.

Benny was beaming as he rushed to bring

cold drinks to the players. It was so much fun being part of the team! It was nearly the end of the fifth inning, and the Bears were leading six to five. "We're going to win," he said under his breath. "We're the best!"

Michael took a big gulp of cool water and splashed some on his face. He felt hot, tired, and dirty, but he was having the time of his life. He was really happy that he and Nicole had met the Aldens. They had found such great friends.

"All we have to do is hold the lead," Coach Warren said to Henry and Chuck a little later. It was a close game, and Henry hoped the Bears would win.

The last inning passed in a blur, and when Nicole caught a fly ball for the last out, the Bears cheered. The Bears had won, eight to seven. "Hooray!" Jessie and Violet ran over to Nicole and threw their arms around her, jumping up and down. "Great catch!" Violet said.

Nicole beamed. "We really did it, didn't we?" She felt breathless and a little dizzy.

"We sure did!" Jessie cried.

Soon the rest of the team ran over, jumping up and down and cheering. They were very pleased with themselves. As they walked off the field, Benny said, "You should see Chuck. He's smiling from ear to ear!"

"So's Coach Warren," Michael offered. He lowered his voice. "When are we going to spring the trap?"

Henry moved closer. He knew that Michael was talking about the baseball card in the glove compartment. "We're going to start the party as soon as everyone cleans up."

Half an hour later, the Pirates had left the parking lot, and the Bears were milling around the field, sipping cold lemonade. Henry was just about to approach Coach Warren when a female voice rang out.

"Surprise, surprise!" Violet and Jessie turned to see Mrs. Sealy bearing down on them with a large birthday cake. "I hope Coach Warren can blow out all these candles," she said, teasing. She was balancing the cake carefully, and Jessie noticed that it was decorated to look like a baseball diamond.

Susan and her mother were right behind her, carrying napkins and paper plates.

"Did you know your aunt was planning this?" Violet asked quietly.

Susan looked a little embarrassed. "My aunt knew we were having a party to celebrate after the game, and she decided to bake a cake." She paused. "I'm surprised she knew it was the Coach's birthday. . . ."

Violet didn't say anything. Somehow, Mrs. Sealy always seemed to be in the middle of things.

A little bit later, after the cake had been cut, Violet wandered over to Henry. He was standing next to the van, his hand on the door handle. "Is the baseball card still there?" she said, glancing at the inside of the van.

Henry shook his head. "It's gone," he told her. "Just as I knew it would be."

"So the thief is right here!" It gave Violet a little chill to think that the thief was someone close by — someone so close she could almost reach out and touch him or her. She glanced around the field. Chuck was sitting next to Mr. Jackson in the dugout, eating cake, and Mrs. Sealy was talking to Coach Warren. Susan had been collecting signatures on a giant birthday card, and she made her way over to Violet and Henry.

"We can give this to the coach just as soon as you two sign it," she said. After Henry and Violet wrote their names, she headed for Coach Warren. Henry motioned for the rest of the Aldens to follow him.

"We'd like to wish you a happy birthday, Coach," Susan began. As Coach Warren took the card, Henry stepped forward.

"And we have a little present for you." To Violet's amazement, he took a plastic-wrapped baseball card out of his pocket.

"Why, thank you," Coach Warren said. His face lit up when he recognized Joe DiMaggio.

"How in the world . . ." Violet muttered.

Jessie edged closer. "That's the real card," she said in a low voice. "Henry substituted a fake one in the glove compartment to catch the thief."

"What do we do now?" Violet whispered.

"We spring the trap," Jessie said simply.

She moved quickly and stood between Susan and Coach Warren. "There's something you need to know, Coach," she began. "You know the series of thefts we've been having. . . ."

The coach nodded sadly. "I had hoped all that was behind us."

"I'm afraid it's not," Henry said firmly. "In fact, someone tried to steal your birthday present today. The Joe DiMaggio card."

The coach fingered the baseball card. "Are you sure?"

"I'm positive. That's why we set a trap and substituted a fake card in the glove compartment of the van." Everyone in the crowd was very still. Violet noticed that Chuck jammed his hands in his pockets, and Mr. Jackson looked worried. "And someone is holding the fake card right now. . . ."

"But who would do such a thing?" Susan blurted out. She looked at her aunt, who was fumbling with her pocketbook.

"I think it's you, Mrs. Sealy," Henry said quietly. "I saw you poking around the van earlier today. You had no reason to be there."

"This is ridiculous!" Mrs. Sealy blurted out. She clutched her pocketbook more firmly, and suddenly Violet realized that she had something to hide.

"How dare you accuse my sister!" Mrs. Miller said. "What would she want with a baseball card? Look, I'll prove it to you." Before anyone could stop her, she grabbed Mrs. Sealy's pocketbook and emptied the contents on a picnic table. "See, what did I tell you?" she said angrily. "Here's a hairbrush, some tissues, a change purse, and . . ." She paused, shaken. A plastic-wrapped baseball card lay squarely on the table. "Oh, no!" she gasped.

"And a baseball card," Henry said. He picked up the card and showed it to the group. "Joe DiMaggio. Except this one's not autographed."

Mrs. Miller looked astonished. "What's going on?" she asked, turning to her sister. Mrs. Sealy didn't answer, and stood with her arms folded across her chest. "Well, say something, Edna," Mrs. Miller persisted. "How did this end up in your purse?"

Mrs. Sealy hesitated for a moment, and then realized the game was up. "All right," she said. Her voice was low and angry. "I took the card."

"And that's not all you took, is it?" Jessie asked.

Mrs. Sealy shook her head. "I took some other things as well."

"But *why?*" Susan looked as if she was near tears. "Why would you do such a thing?" Violet felt sorry for her. It must be terrible to think that your own aunt would try to destroy your team.

"You know I wanted you to drop out of baseball," Mrs. Sealy began. "I thought if enough bad things happened, maybe you'd get disgusted and stop playing. Or maybe Coach would disband the Bears, I don't know . . ." Her voice trailed off. "I don't suppose this makes sense to you."

"No, it doesn't," Susan said. Her voice was shaky. "I love being on the team. And I never understood why you hate the game so much."

"Don't you see?" Mrs. Sealy took a step

toward Susan. "It takes time away from more important things. You could be a wonderful artist if you just spent more time painting. You're wasting your time on this . . . baseball field."

"Why didn't you just tell her how you felt?" Mrs. Miller asked.

Mrs. Sealy looked vaguely at her sister. "I tried to . . . I guess I never believed it would sink in. I thought this way would be better."

"You made a big mistake," Coach Warren said. "You've caused a lot of problems for us."

"I know. I see now that I was wrong." She paused. "I'm really sorry, Susan. You probably don't believe this, but I did it for you."

"But I wasn't giving up my painting," Susan said. Her voice was stronger now. "I'm still going to take lessons and paint every day in the off-season. I thought you knew that."

Mrs. Sealy shook her head and for a moment no one said anything.

"It's a big relief to know who did it," Chuck said.

"Did you take Jessie's mitt?" Benny demanded. "And then try to trick her with a fake one?"

"Yes, I took her mitt." Mrs. Sealy looked embarrassed. "But I don't know anything about a fake one."

"You don't?" Henry looked suspicious.

"She's telling the truth," Chuck said. "I felt so sorry for you, Jessie, that I tried to make you a new one. I guess I didn't fool anyone."

"*You* did?" asked Jessie. Chuck nodded, embarrassed.

"The new one still looked new," Jessie explained.

Benny turned to Mr. Jackson. "We were afraid maybe you were the one who switched gloves."

"Me?" Mr. Jackson looked surprised. "What made you think that?"

"You always keep a saltshaker in the dugout . . ."

"And salt can be used to make new leather look old," Violet finished for him.

Mr. Jackson laughed. "Well, I can explain the saltshaker to you. Hard-boiled eggs. I love 'em. Eat 'em all the time." He grinned. "But what's a hard-boiled egg without salt? Anyway, why would I want to hurt the team?"

"You said you didn't think girls should be on the team," said Benny.

"Well," Mr. Jackson said, "I'm beginning to realize I was wrong about that. Very wrong." He looked at Jessie and she smiled.

"But I saw you snooping around the lockers one day," Benny said. "You said they needed painting, but I knew they didn't."

"Oh, that." Mr. Jackson was embarrassed. "I have a little confession to make, Benny. I was trying to sneak Stockings back into your locker, but you caught me."

"Stockings! You found Stockings?" Benny was thrilled. He had his teddy bear back.

Mr. Jackson nodded. "My little granddaughter picked him up, Benny. But I was afraid everyone would think I'd stolen the other missing things."

"What about the bat?" Susan said suddenly. "How come I ended up with Ann's bat?"

"I'm responsible for that," Mrs. Sealy said. "I thought that if they suspected you of taking it, they'd throw you off the team."

"Edna! That was a *terrible* thing to do," Susan's mother said.

"I know." Mrs. Sealy stared at the ground. She looked very sad.

"Where's my glove?" Jessie spoke up. "I hope you didn't sell it!"

"It's in the trunk of my car," Mrs. Sealy said. "We can get it right now."

They walked silently to the parking lot, and Mrs. Sealy opened the trunk of her car and handed Jessie her glove.

Jessie thrust her hand inside it. She felt the little rough spot inside. This was the real glove from Aunt Jane!

"I think I better leave now," Mrs. Sealy said quietly. Everyone was watching her except Mrs. Miller, who had her arm around Susan.

"Wait, there's still something I don't understand," Jessie said. "What did you mean when you said that Coach Warren was in for the surprise of his life? I thought you and Mr. Jackson were plotting something."

"No, for once I wasn't plotting anything," Mrs. Sealy said. "Just a surprise birthday party."

"Something else is bothering me." Nicole stepped out of the crowd. "Did you cut the cables in the van that day?"

"Yes, I did." Mrs. Sealy's voice was so low Nicole could hardly hear her. "I wanted you to miss the first game of the season. I'll pay for the repairs."

"I suppose you took the keys to my van, too," Coach Warren said angrily.

Mrs. Sealy nodded.

"We thought *you* took them," Jessie said quietly to Chuck.

"And we thought you got lost on purpose, too," Michael added.

Chuck took off his baseball cap and ran his fingers through his hair. "No, I'm afraid I'm just lousy at directions."

"Who was that boy we saw you with in

the store?" Benny asked. "He plays for the Pirates."

"Oh, that's my little brother, Danny," Chuck said.

"You have a brother who plays baseball!" Jessie exclaimed. "Why didn't you tell us about him?"

"I was going to tell you about him when the season was over. I thought you might think it was kind of strange that he was playing for the other team." He paused for a moment. "You see, Danny joined the Pirates way before I started working for Coach Warren."

"We've certainly cleared up a lot of things," Henry said.

"I'm really sorry," Mrs. Sealy said in a small voice. "I just wanted Susan to quit the team." She looked so miserable, everyone felt sorry for her.

"Well, we all make mistakes," Coach Warren said gruffly. "Maybe we should just forget this one." Everyone was quiet while Mrs. Sealy started the car and pulled out of the parking lot.

"I'm glad that's over!" Chuck said, letting out a long breath.

"I'm glad that you figured out what was going on," Coach Warren said to the Aldens.

"I think we should try to put this behind us," Chuck said.

An hour later, the Aldens were celebrating with Michael and Nicole on the front porch of Grandfather's house. Benny was hugging Stockings tightly. Violet looked at her little brother and smiled.

"Things have a way of turning out all right, don't they?" she said. They had solved the mystery, and she had even hit a home run!

Jessie nodded. "Benny got Stockings back, and I got my autographed glove back."

"And we won the game!" Michael added. He remembered how exciting it had been.

"Do you think Susan will be okay?" Nicole asked. "I really feel sorry for her."

"I think she'll be fine," Henry said. "She knows her aunt made a big mistake, but it's all over with now." It was a warm evening, and Mrs. McGregor's garden was starting to bloom. "You know, we really did a good job today. We won the game and we solved another mystery."

"*Another* mystery?" Nicole asked curiously.

"Do you mean you've done this before?" Michael piped up.

Jessie laughed. "Many times."

"Wow," Nicole said softly. "Can you tell us about them?"

"Sure," Benny told her. "But it'll take a long time!"

GERTRUDE CHANDLER WARNER discovered when she was teaching that many readers who like an exciting story could find no books that were both easy and fun to read. She decided to try to meet this need, and her first book, *The Boxcar Children*, quickly proved she had succeeded.

Miss Warner drew on her own experiences to write the mystery. As a child she spent many hours watching trains go by on the tracks opposite her family home. She often dreamed about what it would be like to set up housekeeping in a caboose or freight car — the situation the Alden children find themselves in.

When Miss Warner received requests for more adventures involving Henry, Jessie, Violet, and Benny Alden, she began additional stories. In each, she chose a special setting and introduced unusual or eccentric characters who liked the unpredictable.

While the mystery element is central to each of Miss Warner's books, she never thought of them as strictly juvenile mysteries. She liked to stress the Aldens' independence and resourcefulness and their solid New England devotion to using up and making do. The Aldens go about most of their adventures with as little adult supervision as possible—something else that delights young readers.

Miss Warner lived in Putnam, Connecticut, until her death in 1979. During her lifetime, she received hundreds of letters from girls and boys telling her how much they liked her books.

PLAY BALL!

In case *you* can't get to a ball park, Henry, Jessie, Violet, and Benny are sending the baseball fun straight to your home plate! Just try your hand at these baseball puzzles and activities. The Alden kids are certain you'll agree, they're a hit!

What an A-maze-ing Catch!

It's a line drive to the outfield. Which of these three players will catch the ball? Follow the squiggly lines and you will see!

Hey! Who Turned on the Lights?

There's nothing more fun than climbing into the bleachers to watch a great night game! Here's a different kind of night game for you to try. Just match each of the players to his or her shadow.

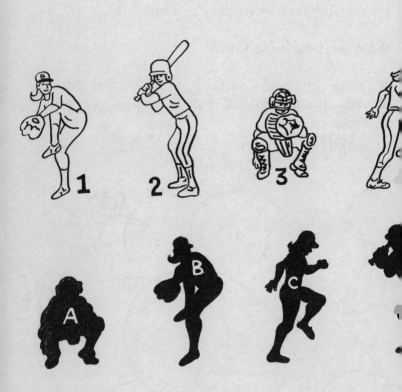

Benny's Ball Search

Lucky Benny! He gets to be batboy for the team. Part of his job is to gather all the balls that might be needed in the big game. There are fifteen balls hidden in this picture. Can you help Benny find them all?

Error in the Field!

At first these two baseball scenes might look like they are from the same game. But if you look closely, you will see these two pictures are not the same at all! Can you find six things that are different between the two pictures?

Going Batty

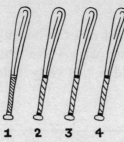

1   2   3   4

Oh dear! Someone has taken Ann's bat. The Aldens
have all gone out to look for it. They've all found
bats, but only one is really Ann's. Find the one that
is different.

Hidden Equipment

There's a piece of baseball equipment in each of these
sentences. Can you find the word you need to play
a game? Just to show what good sports we are, we've
done the first one for you!

Sure, you can pet She*ba. Ll*amas are very sweet
creatures, you know.

Don't listen to him. It takes more than talent to make
you a good hitter!

I'm sorry, Eric, appointments are necessary if you
want to meet with the coach.

Okay, team! In order to win, I'll need your help.
Later, I'll take you all out for ice cream.

You like my hair? It's because I found a new comb
at the drugstore.

Nine to a Side

Baseball is a game of nines. There are nine innings in a game, and nine players to a team. To find out the name of the Alden kids' team, color in the spaces that equal nine.

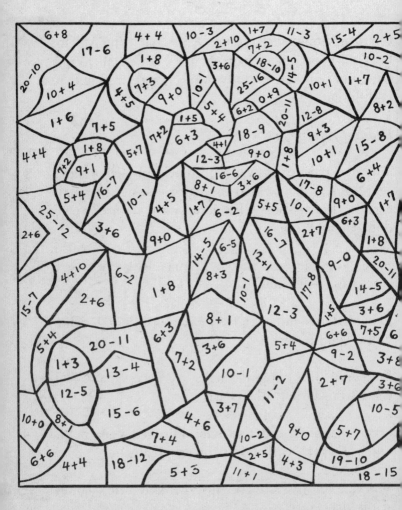

Hip! Hip! Hooray!

Jessie and Violet's team has finally beaten another team! Now it's time to celebrate. Study this team picture very carefully. Then turn the page and take the memory test.

Circle the picture in each row that is exactly the same as the one on the previous page.

The Major League Word Search

The names of thirteen major league baseball teams are hidden in this wordsearch. Look, up, down, diagonally, sideways, and backwards until you find them all.

Words for this puzzle: YANKEES, METS, EXPOS, TIGERS, ASTROS, PHILLIES, BRAVES, RED SOX, ANGELS, BLUE JAYS, REDS, PADRES, CUBS

```
Y M O N C N T A N D
A C Y U T A S H A B
P L B R A V E S U A
A S X E W Y R W S A
D S V M B A S T E S
R O O E H N S I I T
E P S T R K R G L R
S X O S D E R E L O
L E G F P E D R I S
A N G E L S O S H I
S Y A J E U L B P W
```

Up at the Snack Bar!

Just mix and eat these baseball treats!

Stadium Pretzels

You will need
2 packages of dry yeast
1½ cups warm water
2 tablespoons sugar
1 teaspoon salt
4 cups flour
1 egg, beaten
coarse salt

Here's what you do (with the help of a grown-up):
Mix together all the ingredients except the coarse salt and egg. Knead mixture until it becomes rubbery like dough. Pull off small pieces and roll into different lengths. On cookie sheet, twist lengths of dough into pretzel shapes — or any shapes you'd like. Coat your pretzels with the beaten egg, then sprinkle on coarse salt. Place the pretzel dough in the oven and bake your pretzels for 10–15 minutes at 425 degrees.

Hot Dog! No-Cook Hot Dogs!

You will need:
2 slices thinly sliced bologna
2 slices thinly sliced salami
2 slices thinly sliced cheese
1 hot dog bun
mustard or ketchup

Here's what you do:
Pile all of the slices together, with the cheese slices on the top of the pile. Carefully roll the slices together tightly so they look like a hot dog. Place your hot dot in the hot dog bun. Top with mustard or ketchup just as you would a regular ballpark hot dog.

Terrific Team Pennants

Show your team spirit! Wave these super team flags at the ballpark — or in front of your TV!

You will need:
scissors
poster board
a picture of your favorite major league or local team's emblem (this can be hand-drawn or cut out of a magazine)
glue
markers
white felt

Here's what you do:
Cut a long triangle from the poster board. Glue your team's emblem to the triangle. Use the markers to write your favorite team's name next to the emblem. Cut the felt into small strips. Fold them in half and glue them to the back of your pennant. Be sure to glue them close to the edge of the pennant so that they stick out.

Answers to the Puzzles

What an A-maze-ing Catch!

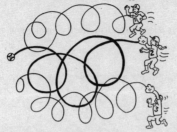

Hey! Who Turned on the Lights?

1-B; 2-D; 3-A; 4-C

Benny's Ball Search

Error in the Field

Going Batty

Number one is different

Hidden Equipment

Sure, you can pet She*ba*. *Ll*amas are very sweet creatures, you know.

Don't listen to hi*m*. *It t*akes more than talent to make you a good hitter!

I'm sorry, Eri*c*, *ap*pointments are necessary if you want to meet with the coach.

Okay, team! In order to win, I'll need your hel*p*. *Late*r, I'll take you all out for ice cream.

You like my hair? It's because I found a new com*b at* the drugstore.

Nine to a Side

Hip! Hip! Hooray!

The Major League Word Search